Barbie Mariposa

A Junior Novelization

Adapted by Shannon Penney
Based on the Original Screenplay by Elise Allen

SCHOLASTIC INC.

New York   Toronto   London   Auckland   Sydney
Mexico City   New Delhi   Hong Kong   Buenos Aires

ISBN-13: 978-0-545-03590-3
ISBN-10: 0-545-03590-2

BARBIE™ as Mariposa™ and associated trademarks and trade dress are owned by, and used under license from, Mattel, Inc. Copyright © 2008 Mattel, Inc. All Rights Reserved.

Photography by The Mattel Photo Studio
Book design by Angela Jun
Special thanks to Rob Hudnut, Tiffany J. Shuttleworth, Vicki Jaeger, Monica Okazaki, Luke Carroll, Anita Lee, Julie Puckrin, Walter Martishius, Derek Goodfellow, Pam Prostarr, Aeron Kline, Conrad Chow, Lester Chung, Allan Pantoja, Kelsey Ayukawa, Eric Wong, Greg Montgomery, Ryan Singh, Sarah Miyashita, Winston Fan, Karl Bildstein, Sean Newton

Published by Scholastic Inc.
SCHOLASTIC and associated logos are trademarks and/or registered trademarks of Scholastic Inc.

12 11 10 9 8 7 6 5 4 3 2 1   8 9 10/0

Printed in the U.S.A.
First printing, March 2008

Introduction

The night sky over Fairytopia was speckled with glittering stars. Everyone was sleeping in the Magic Meadow. All were quiet . . . except for one.

Bibble the Puffball bustled about in the meadow. He was building models of other Puffballs out of dirt, sticks, and flowers.

"Dizzle," Bibble sighed, adding a final purple flower to the last Puffball.

Bibble was going to visit Dizzle and he

was nervous that he wouldn't fit in with Dizzle's friends.

Bibble decided to practice how he should act in front of the model Puffballs.

Bibble walked by the Puffballs, nodding at them casually, trying to act carefree. When he reached the model of Dizzle, he leaned on her arm. But the fake Puffball couldn't support him!

CRASH!

Dizzle's model toppled over into the Puffball next to it. Before Bibble could do anything, all five Puffballs had collapsed into piles of dirt, sticks, and flowers.

Just then, a voice came from inside a nearby Peony. "Bibble?" Elina, Bibble's fairy friend, flew out of her flower home. "Bibble? What are you doing? Come inside."

Bibble jumped up, surprised by Elina. "Oh, uh, okay!" he cried.

Elina smiled. "Are you excited about visiting Dizzle?"

Bibble sighed, shrugging. "I'm canceling the trip."

"What?" Elina asked, surprised. "Why would you do that? You were so excited to meet all of Dizzle's friends!"

"Exactly — her friends!" Bibble's head dropped. "What if they don't like me? What if they think I'm too goofy, or not cool enough, or —"

"Oh, I see," Elina interrupted. "You're worried that you won't fit in." She looked at her Puffball friend closely. Poor Bibble! Suddenly, Elina had an idea. "I think I can help. Let me tell you a story about a good friend of mine. Her name is Mariposa, and she's a Butterfly Fairy. . . ."

Chapter 1

In the land of Fairytopia, there was a distant realm called Flutterfield. Flutterfield was a beautiful fairy city.

Flutterfield was completely cut off from the rest of Fairytopia because it was surrounded by hungry Skeezites. Skeezites were terrible flying beasts that liked to eat the Butterfly Fairies! They were afraid of the light, so the fairies were safe during the day. But at night, the Skeezites circled Flutterfield, searching for their next meal.

For centuries, the Butterfly Fairies had to hide when the sun went down. Every night, they feared being found by the Skeezites.

But one day, a magical fairy named Marabella filled the trees with beautiful glowing flowers. The flowers were enchanted and would shine for as long as Marabella lived.

Marabella was made queen and from that day on Flutterfield was always bright. The fairies were safe from Skeezites if they stayed within the city's borders. And every Butterfly Fairy was happy to follow that rule. . . .

Except one.

Mariposa was a beautiful, curious Butterfly Fairy. She loved her home but couldn't help wondering what was beyond the city's borders.

One night, Mariposa was sitting on a leaf at the edge of Flutterfield as she often did. She was gazing up at the stars. They were so beautiful. So peaceful. So —

"Are you kidding me?" A loud, sassy voice cut through the silence.

Mariposa spun around to see her best friend, Willa, flying up behind her. "I thought you were coming with me to the party tonight!"

Mariposa shrugged. "You know me. I'm not good at parties!"

"You could have just hung out with me," Willa said.

"But I can hang out with you here!" Mariposa smiled at her friend. "Come sit — I want to show you something."

"Do I look like a Skeezite snack? I came to get you *away* from the city's edge . . . again!" Willa narrowed her eyes and looked cautiously around her as she made her way to Mariposa's side.

"You'll be fine," Mariposa assured her, reaching out a hand. "It's light enough. Now look up. What do you see?"

Willa gazed up. At first all she could see

were the shadows of Skeezites in the distance. But after a moment she focused on the nighttime sky, filled with millions of twinkling stars. Willa's eyes opened wide.

"It's beautiful, isn't it?" Mariposa asked, smiling. "Sometimes I look for patterns up there. You have to connect the dots between stars. See? There's the Archer." Mariposa pointed out the Archer's belt, then his bow and arrow.

Mariposa showed Willa all sorts of patterns in the sky. "Sometimes I connect the stars to make pictures of places I've only read about in books," she explained.

Willa smiled. "I can see why you like this."

A moment later, a Skeezite swooped over the city! It flew so close, the girls could feel the rush of air from its giant wings. But as it neared the bright city lights it became scared and zipped away.

"I take it back!" Willa cried. "I *don't* see why you like this! Come on — we should get to bed. Besides, if you stay up too late, Rayna and Rayla will be on your case again for sleeping in. I'm sure there will be lots to do tomorrow—as usual."

"You go ahead," Mariposa said. "I'll get to bed soon. And I promise, this time I won't oversleep."

Willa gave her friend one last look, then flew off into the light of the city.

Chapter 2

Willa came to get Mariposa for work the next morning. But rather than being ready to leave, Mariposa was still fast asleep.

"Mariposa? Mariposa!"

Mariposa had overslept — again! She jumped out of bed and rushed to get ready. They were already late for work! She and Willa flew out of the house and through the root neighborhood as fast as their wings would take them.

"Hurry!" Willa cried.

The girls were just around the corner from Rayna and Rayla's house when a friendly fairy named Henna called out to them. Both girls waved. Henna was Queen Marabella's attendant, and all of the fairies liked her!

"Hi!" she said warmly as she reached the girls. "I didn't see you at the party last night, Mariposa. What happened?"

"Oh, nothing," Mariposa said. "I just didn't think I'd have a lot of fun."

Henna looked at her sympathetically. "I understand. I don't always feel like I belong, either."

Mariposa was shocked. "Really? You?"

Henna nodded. "But I'll get where I want to be," she said confidently. "You can, too — just stick with me." With that, she grinned and flew off to join a nearby group of fairies. They all looked happy to see her as they went on their way.

Willa turned back to Mariposa. "There's no chance that Henna ever feels like she doesn't belong. Everyone in Flutterfield loves her — including the queen."

Mariposa nodded. Willa was right. She and Henna were nothing alike.

"Mariposa! Willa! Is that you?" Rayna was calling for them, and she sounded upset!

Mariposa looked at Willa and sighed. "We're on our way," she called as they hurried to get to work.

Chapter 3

"You're late!" Rayna cried as Mariposa and Willa flew into sight.

"I'm sorry," Mariposa said. "I overslept, and then —"

Rayna held up her hand. "Not interested! There's a ball at the palace tonight, and we already made a list of everything we need."

Rayla handed over the list, and Willa and Mariposa took a look. "Thistleburst?" Mariposa asked.

"To braid in our hair so it will sparkle like the stars," Rayna explained.

Willa grimaced. "But Thistleburst only grows deep underground in the Nettle Swamp. It smells there!"

"Well, we're worth it," Rayla finished for her.

Willa rolled her eyes and flew off, leaving Mariposa alone with the two sisters. Mariposa did her best to help the spoiled sisters get ready for the ball. It didn't take her long to figure out why they wanted to look their best.

"I need you to shine my wings," Rayna insisted, pulling Mariposa toward a mirror.

"No," Rayla said, grabbing Mariposa's other arm and pulling her the other way. "I need you to perfume my hair. We need to

be perfect for the prince tonight!"

Mariposa was puzzled. "But I thought the prince never went out in public," she said.

"True," Rayna replied. "So when he does go out, it will be to fall in love — with me."

"Or me!" Rayla chimed in.

Mariposa spritzed the scent from a

flower into Rayla's hair. "But how do you know you'll fall in love with the prince?"

"He's a prince," Rayla said matter-of-factly. "That means he's special."

Just then, Rayna's squeal came from the other side of the room. "Mariposa, I have absolutely nothing to wear!" she cried.

Mariposa looked over to Rayna's closet. It was overflowing with beautiful dresses. "But, Rayna," she said, "your wardrobe is full."

"Of dresses that aren't befluttered! How can I know which is best until you beflutter them all?"

Mariposa picked out as many of the sisters' dresses as she could carry. Struggling with her load, she stumbled into another chamber where a bunch of flowers was hanging. She nudged the flowers with her hip and a group of tiny and adorable Flutterpixies peeked out from among the petals. Almost immediately the Flutterpixies set to work — humming as they went — and before long the dresses were sparkling magnificently. They had hardly finished when Rayna and Rayla began grabbing at the dresses greedily.

"I love it!" Rayla cried, trying on one dress.

"Yes! I will look gorgeous in this!" Rayna added, studying herself in the mirror.

Mariposa thanked the Flutterpixies for their work and turned to watch the sisters admiring their reflections. "Can I ask you guys something?" she asked hesitantly. "Do you ever feel like you don't belong?"

Rayna and Rayla stared at Mariposa,

considering her question. Then they burst out laughing.

"Why would we?" Rayna giggled. The sisters glanced at each other and burst into laughter again.

Mariposa hung her head and slipped outside.

In a dark lair deep in the root neighborhood of Flutterfield, the queen's attendant, Henna, was all alone in front of a boiling vat. She carefully stirred the liquid inside and with each bit she added, a puff of smoke rose from the cauldron. "What do you do when it's not enough to just be you?" Henna asked in a sing-songy voice. "You steal the me you want to be!" Henna grinned. She leaned over and ladled some of the potion into a glass vial.

"So long, Queen Marabella," she cackled. "It's time for your servant to get the respect she deserves."

And with that, Henna placed the top on the vial of potion and put it in her pocket.

Chapter 4

All of Flutterfield was excited about the palace ball. The palace looked beautiful in the glow of Queen Marabella's magical lights.

Many fairies arrived dressed in their finest clothing. Among them were Rayna and Rayla, followed by Willa and Mariposa. Rayna and Rayla looked lovely! Willa had brought back some shimmering Thistleburst for their hair, and though it was horrible to collect, the Thistleburst gave off a fabulous sparkle.

The sisters flew inside, each trying to beat the other to the door, and Willa followed.

Mariposa stayed behind but didn't go far in case she was needed. She watched the other fairies as they filed into the palace. They all looked so fancy! She recognized Lord Gastrous, Queen Marabella's chief advisor, on his way in. He was boasting to a group of fairies of how he'd once rescued Flutterfield from disaster.

"Impressive," a voice behind Mariposa said. Mariposa turned to see Henna. "At least it would be if it ever actually happened. Gastrous has never dealt with anything tougher than deciding what to eat for breakfast."

She smiled and gestured to the palace door. "Are you coming in?"

Mariposa shook her head. "No, thanks. I think I'll stay out here."

"Okay," Henna replied, grinning. "But remember what I told you — stick with me and I can get you everything you want."

Henna turned to go, but as she did, a glass vial slipped from her pocket and clattered to the ground. Mariposa bent to scoop it up. She called out to Henna and flew over to return it.

"Thanks," Henna said as she retrieved the vial and flew off.

Mariposa watched her go, then pulled out her book. She flew into the air, reading as she went. But she wasn't paying attention to her flying. Before she knew it, she bumped right into a male fairy who was also flying with his nose buried in a book.

"Oh, I'm so sorry!" she cried. "I'm such a klutz. I got lost in my book, and I — wait a minute. Are you . . . you are!" said Mariposa, pointing. "You're reading the same book that I am!" She held up her book to show him.

The other fairy looked down at his book and smiled. "You're right. It's my favorite. I've read it nine times."

"I've read it *ten* times!" Mariposa laughed.

"Wow . . . what do you like about it?"

"Well," answered Mariposa, "it's not safe to leave Flutterfield, but when I read I get to visit the entire universe."

The fairy looked at her thoughtfully.

"Most Butterfly Fairies I know aren't interested in the rest of the universe. Are you here for the ball?"

"Sort of," Mariposa responded. "But I'm not really comfortable at parties."

"I feel the same way!" the male fairy said.

"You do?" Mariposa asked, and the other fairy nodded. "I'm Mariposa."

"I'm, uh, Andreyus."

Mariposa smiled. "Really? The same name as the hero in this book?"

Andreyus smiled back. "Maybe that's why I like the book so much," he replied.

Mariposa could have talked to Andreyus for much longer, but soon she heard Rayna and Rayla calling for her. As she turned to leave, Andreyus said, "I hope to see you again."

"Me, too!" said Mariposa.

❧   ❧   ❧

After the ball, Mariposa headed home. In the middle of the night, she woke to a loud knocking on her window. Who could it be?

"Mariposa!" came a whisper from the other side of the window. "It's me."

"Andreyus?" Mariposa asked. It sounded like the fairy she'd bumped into earlier.

Mariposa opened the window and Andreyus came in quickly. Something was clearly wrong.

"I'm so sorry," he whispered. "I didn't mean to startle you. I'm not who you think I am. I am Prince Carlos, and I need your help."

Mariposa couldn't believe her ears. But just then, a loud and urgent knocking sounded at the door.

Prince Carlos moved silently to the other side of the room. "That's the Royal Guard. They're after me!"

The prince quickly explained that the queen had fallen ill that night. He believed it was Ilios poisoning. Most fairies in Flutterfield didn't think that Ilios existed, but Prince Carlos knew nothing else could make the queen so sick. She would die within two days if they didn't do something!

Lord Gastrous had sent the Royal Guard to lock up Prince Carlos for his own protection. In doing so, he would keep the prince from going after the Ilios antidote and putting himself in danger. But without the antidote, the queen would die and the Flutterfield lights would go out!

There was more knocking on the door. "Hello!" came a loud voice. "I need you to open up!"

"One moment, please," Mariposa called, trying to sound calm.

The prince handed Mariposa a map. "I am giving you a map to the Ilios antidote. If the guards catch me, you'll need to follow it. It's our only chance to help the queen!"

The guard continued pounding on the door.

"Why me?" Mariposa asked hurriedly.

"You're the only other fairy I've met who reads, who understands the world outside Flutterfield. It has to be you." With that, Prince Carlos hid in the shadows just as the Royal Guard burst into the room.

As the guard searched the room for the prince, Prince Carlos slipped out the door unseen. Once the guard was satisfied that the prince was not there, he left and Mariposa found herself alone once more, holding the prince's map in her hand.

Chapter 5

The next morning, Willa and Mariposa flew through Flutterfield on their way to work. Willa had just heard about the queen's illness.

"Everyone says that the queen has been poisoned, but nobody knows how," she said.

Mariposa frowned. "Is anyone talking about Ilios poison? It's not supposed to exist, but —"

"Queen Marabella is sick with something *real*," Willa interrupted.

When the girls arrived at Rayna and Rayla's house, Rayna was already calling for them. The sisters had big plans to throw a "Get Well, Marabella" party that very night! Rayna handed Willa a list of the things they needed, including more Thistleburst. Willa flew off, grumbling, to find the items on the list.

As Mariposa started to get the house ready for the party, Rayla burst inside.

"Prince Carlos has been locked up in the palace!" she cried. "Everyone says it's for his own protection . . . which means he's in *danger*!"

Rayna gasped. "That's so romantic!"

Mariposa grew pale and sank down into a chair. Rayna and Rayla looked at her, confused.

Mariposa took a deep breath. She told

them everything and even showed them the map that Prince Carlos had given her.

Rayna immediately grabbed the map, intrigued. "Are you thinking what I'm thinking?" she asked Rayla.

Rayla studied the map over Rayna's shoulder. "We are going to get the antidote!"

"What?!" cried Mariposa in disbelief.

"You don't really think someone like you can be trusted to rescue the queen, do you?" Rayna scoffed at Mariposa. "You'll come with us, of course, to carry our snacks and things. We'll need Fluttercorn, Fairy Cakes . . . I will make you a list!"

"But we will be the ones to save Flutterfield, win the queen's gratitude, and get the greatest reward — the prince!"

Rayla added with certainty.

Mariposa shook her head. "But the map leads out of Flutterfield, into Skeezite territory."

"We'll just make it back before dark, then," Rayna said matter-of-factly. "Easy."

Mariposa didn't have a choice. She packed their things and the three fairies set out across Flutterfield.

At the city's edge Mariposa checked the map. "We need to go to the center of the Bewilderness, where we'll find a white flower. That must be the antidote."

Rayla frowned. "I've never been outside the city." She and Rayna suddenly looked nervous.

Mariposa took a deep breath and bravely led the way beyond the city limit.

Mariposa, Rayna, and Rayla traveled all day. Before long, it was dusk. The longer they traveled, the more irritated the sisters became. They argued nonstop! Mariposa did her best to keep Rayna and Rayla calm.

As the last bit of light left the sky, they heard a loud sound.

"Skeezites!" the sisters screamed together.

The fairies dove behind a row of bushes as two Skeezites appeared. They were close enough for the girls to hear, and they mumbled and grumbled about how hungry they were. Hungry for Butterfly Fairies! The girls had to move fast, before they were discovered.

Mariposa plucked some large flowers. She handed one each to Rayna and Rayla, and kept one for herself. "Carry these," she instructed. "Skeezites rely on smell. If they smell the flowers and not us, they won't know we're here." Luckily, Mariposa had learned this in a book!

The girls flew off, holding the flowers in front of them. They could hear the two Skeezites mumbling, "*Mmmm*, I smell pretty flowers!"

Rayna checked the map as they flew,

peering at it in the starlight. She looked at it so closely, in fact, that she didn't see a tree trunk in front of her and she went tumbling through the air. Rayna and the map went one way . . . and the flower went another!

"I smell fairy!" one Skeezite yelled.

"*Butterfly* Fairy!" the other chimed in.

Mariposa and Rayla dropped their flowers and swooped in just in time, grabbing Rayna by the arms. But in their hurry to save their friend, they left the map behind. A Skeezite chomped down where Rayna had been only seconds before! He caught the map in his teeth, chewed, and swallowed. The map was destroyed!

The girls didn't have time to worry about the map. Skeezites were after them! As the fairies zipped through the air, swooping and darting, more and more Skeezites joined the chase.

"Where do we go?" Rayla cried.

"All the landmarks were on the map!" said Rayna.

Mariposa had to think fast! "Wait!" she suddenly said. "I remember something from the map. On our route was the picture of a rising sun."

Rayla groaned. "But we can't follow the sun. It's dark!"

"No, don't you see?" Mariposa continued to fly along quickly. "The sun rises in the east. If the sun is in our path, we need to fly east."

"So we just need to find out which way east is," Rayna said, panicking more and more. "Which we can only do *with the map!*"

Mariposa looked up at the sky. "No, we can use the Archer — in the stars! His arrow always points east." She quickly found the Archer in the stars, and all three fairies turned to fly in the direction his arrow pointed. But before long, they had two big problems.

The Skeezites were still flying right behind them.

And ahead there was a thick wall of thorny bushes!

Mariposa had to do something, and fast. She quickly led the way and the three girls zoomed through a small space between the thorny branches and crossed to the other side.

One by one, the Skeezites crashed into the wall of thorns. They were too big to fit through!

Mariposa, Rayna, and Rayla all breathed huge sighs of relief. They were safe . . . for now.

Chapter 6

Back in Flutterfield, Willa returned to Rayna and Rayla's house with the Thistleburst. But the sisters were nowhere to be seen. Where had they gone? And where was Mariposa?

A Flutterpixie came to meet Willa and handed her a note. "'Went to save the queen,'" she read out loud. "'Try to contact Prince Carlos. He'll tell you everything.'"

Willa's eyes widened. She had to find the prince!

Meanwhile, at the palace, Prince Carlos was locked inside a cage. How would he be able to save the queen now?

"Guard!" he called.

After a long moment, Lord Gastrous appeared in the doorway. "You called, Your Highness?"

Prince Carlos was obviously upset. "I command you to release me!"

Lord Gastrous shook his head. "I'm sorry, but I can't do that. If the queen doesn't get well, Flutterfield needs you to be here, safe and ready to rule. I can't have you off risking your life, looking for a cure for a poison that doesn't exist." With that, he sighed, turned, and left the room.

"Lord Gastrous!" Carlos shouted after him. But the prince was alone. "Mariposa, I hope you're in better shape than I am," he whispered.

❧   ❧   ❧

Willa flew to the palace and began peeking in windows. She had no idea how she would find the prince, but she knew she had to try. As she passed the window of the room where the sick queen lay, she heard voices.

"I brought her favorite brushes and ribbons," came Henna's voice.

Ducking into the shadows so she wouldn't be seen, Willa peered into the room.

Lord Gastrous and Henna were just arriving and Henna carried a large basket.

"The queen always loves it when I do her hair," Henna was saying. "I thought maybe it would help."

Lord Gastrous gave her a small smile.

"You're a good friend, Henna."

Henna began softly brushing Queen Marabella's hair. "Has there been any change?" she asked.

Lord Gastrous shook his head. "The prince keeps talking about Ilios. You don't think there's the slightest chance . . ."

Henna sighed. "I wish as much as anyone that we could help the queen, but everyone knows that Ilios doesn't exist." She looked down at Marabella, and her eyes filled with tears.

"You're right," Lord Gastrous said. "It's ridiculous, of course."

"Perhaps you should check on the prince," Henna suggested.

"Yes," agreed Lord Gastrous. "You're right. The minute you know something, let me know." He gave Henna a small nod, cast one more pained look at the queen, and left the room.

Henna looked sympathetically down at the queen as she brushed her hair. Then she leaned closer, and poured some of the potion from her vial into the queen's mouth.

"Not long now, Queen Marabella," Henna said softly. "Soon I will rule all of Flutterfield."

Willa was shocked as she saw the evil grin on Henna's face. She quickly left to continue her search for the prince.

❧   ❧   ❧

Night fell in Flutterfield and Queen Marabella's illness began to take its toll. As her magic faded, so did the lights that protected the city.

Willa flew close to the remaining lights.

Where was Prince Carlos?

Willa spotted Lord Gastrous making his way down a hall and decided to follow him. Soon he came to a door blocked by the castle guards. Willa flew back outside and approached the guarded room's window. Inside she saw the prince in his cage. She caught his attention but he could not understand her through the closed balcony doors.

Suddenly, Lord Gastrous came into the room! Willa darted away from the window and out of sight.

"Is everything okay in here?" Lord Gastrous asked, stepping into the room. "I thought I heard something."

"No, everything is fine," Prince Carlos assured him. "Except . . . I could use some air. Could you open the balcony doors?"

"Prince Carlos, we must keep the doors shut for your own protection."

"Just while you are here. You will be able to protect me," pleaded the prince.

Reluctantly, Lord Gastrous opened the balcony doors. Then he turned back to the prince. "We're doing everything we can to comfort the queen," he said, trying to reassure the prince.

With Lord Gastrous's back to the door, Willa was able to sneak into the room while the prince distracted him.

"But if you let me out, using the key . . ." said the prince, trying to indicate the key on Lord Gastrous's belt to Willa. If she could only get it away from him . . .

"We cannot take the risk," said Lord Gastrous.

"But the key on your belt can free me..."

Suddenly, Willa understood what the prince was trying to tell her. She snuck up behind Lord Gastrous and carefully removed the key to Prince Carlos's cage from his belt. Then she darted to hide until Lord Gastrous was gone.

The prince relaxed, knowing Willa could now free him, and hurried to get Lord Gastrous to depart.

"I understand," he said to Lord Gastrous. "Please let me know if there are any changes in the queen."

Lord Gastrous was surprised that the prince was so easily consoled, but decided to go. He carefully closed the balcony doors and moved to leave. "Of course, Prince Carlos. You will know the second we hear something."

Lord Gastrous left, closing the door

behind him, and Willa approached the cage. "So, you're the prince?" she asked him.

"My name is Carlos," he answered as Willa unlocked his cage. "Are you a friend of Mariposa?"

"Yes. I'm Willa."

"Willa, we must find the antidote for the queen," the prince said urgently.

"First," said Willa, "we have to find out what Henna is up to. I saw her poisoning the queen."

Chapter 7

The next morning, Mariposa, Rayna, and Rayla woke with a start. They had fallen asleep in a clearing after a long, dangerous day. And now it seemed that someone was throwing small seeds at them!

Each girl blamed the others for throwing the seeds, but soon a nearby giggling caught their attention. Silently, the girls flew over toward the giggles. Not far away they found a funny, bunnylike creature with wings. She was rolling with laughter on the ground but disappeared down a hole when she realized the girls had found her.

A moment later she popped up out of different hole, a big smile spreading across her face.

"Hi!" the creature said cheerfully, looking up at the girls. "I'm Zinzie the Meewah!"

"Are you the one throwing seeds at us?" Rayna asked, annoyed.

Zinzie giggled. "It was funny! You should have seen your faces."

"That's not very nice, fooling people that way," Mariposa said.

Zinzie suddenly looked very serious. "I just wanted to play! I don't see anyone out here in the Bewilderness very much, and it gets really lonely. . . ."

"Did you say the Bewilderness?"

Mariposa interrupted.

Zinzie nodded. "That's where we are!"

Mariposa exchanged glances with Ranya and Rayla. Then all three girls cheered.

"We made it!" Rayla cried.

Rayna turned to the little Meewah. "We need you to take us to the center of the Bewilderness."

"But I like you!" Zinzie said, crossing her arms. "I don't want you to go away."

Rayna was about to lose her temper, but Mariposa knew just what to do.

"Zinzie, you like Fluttercorn, right?" she asked. Zinzie nodded enthusiastically.

Zinzie's ears perked up. Her nose twitched. "That heavenly crunch . . . that delectable aroma . . ."

"A whole bag of it," Mariposa said. "And it's all for you, if you want it. But you need to show us the way."

Zinzie darted high into the air and the fairies followed her. Before long, she stopped. "Here we are!" she declared. She took the bag of Fluttercorn from Mariposa and started eating excitedly.

Mariposa, Rayna, and Rayla looked around, confused. They didn't seem to be anywhere special. "*This* is the center of the Bewilderness?" Rayla asked.

"But there's supposed to be a white flower here," Mariposa added.

Rayla paused for a second. "There is — look right here," she said, looking down at the big rock where she saw a picture of a white flower and a mermaid etched into it.

Mariposa studied the picture. "I think this is another map. I think we have to find this mermaid, and she can tell us where the flower is."

"Mermaids live in the Waterwhirls," Zinzie chimed in. "I can take you there."

"And what do you want in return?" Rayna asked, suspicious.

Zinzie grinned. "Fluttercorn, please!"

"Done," Mariposa said, laughing.

🍀　🍀　🍀

Back in Flutterfield, Prince Carlos and Willa had been following Henna, trying to discover her evil plan.

"Are you sure it was Henna who poisoned the queen? We've been following her for hours and she has done nothing out of the ordinary."

"I'm positive," said Willa.

Willa and the prince hid behind a corner and watched as Henna spoke happily with a small group of fairies. But suddenly, she left the group and flew off on her own. The prince and Willa followed her as she disappeared into her lair in the depths of the root neighborhood. Neither Prince Carlos nor Willa had ever seen this place before and it was strange for Henna to be so far from the palace.

"What is she doing down here?"

whispered the prince as he and Henna ducked to stay out of sight. "We must find out." The prince led the way into the lair and a nervous Willa stayed close behind him. When they were able to see into the cave, they were shocked to see Henna talking to a couple of Skeezites!

"You promised us Butterfly Fairy," said one Skeezite to Henna, irritably.

Willa and the prince exchanged horrified looks but stayed quiet.

"Be patient, my little ones. Tonight you will have all the Butterfly Fairies you can eat." The two Skeezites licked their lips and moved closer to Henna. But before they could get too close, she took an orb of bright light from the basket she was holding and held it before her. The Skeezites recoiled in horror. She used the light to guide the

Skeezites farther into the cave and out of sight from Willa and the prince.

"What kind of light was that?" asked Willa in wonder.

"I don't know, but we need to find out. We'll wait for her to leave."

Willa and the prince hid and waited. They were determined to discover what Henna had hidden in the back of her lair. After a long time, they decided they could wait no longer and they crept quietly into the cave. They peeked into a dark room and saw Henna standing over a large cauldron. To their horror, they spotted the two Skeezites sleeping nearby.

"Everyone thinks Ilios doesn't exist," Henna was saying to herself cheerfully. But then she let out a crazy laugh that startled Willa and the prince. They ducked down lower so they would not be seen.

Henna reached to her side and picked up a Thistleburst pod. Then she spooned in some of the liquid from the cauldron. "Who would have thought that a little Ilios and a little Thistleburst would give me so much power?" Henna said with a grin.

Willa and the prince were amazed to see that the moment the Ilios was added to the Thistleburst pod it glowed with a brilliant light. Then Henna began to head for the door, with the glowing Thistleburst pod.

"What a beautiful day to become queen," she said dreamily as she gazed at the light. Then she flew out of her lair without noticing Willa and Prince Carlos.

Determined to stop Henna from seeing her evil plan through, Willa and the prince crept into the lair where the Skeezites were still sound asleep. They were careful not to wake them.

"Now I'll have evidence to show Gastrous," said the prince as he scooped some of the potion out of the cauldron and poured it into a vial. "He'll have to believe me now."

Willa gathered up the Thistleburst that remained unused. "And we can use the light against the Skeezites."

"We'll need more than that," said the prince. "I'll find Gastrous—"

"And I'll go back to the swamp."

The two fairies exchanged determined looks before heading off to accomplish their goals.

Chapter 8

Zinzie led Mariposa, Rayna, and Rayla to the edge of the Waterwhirls, chatting and munching on Fluttercorn all the way.

When they arrived, Mariposa looked down at the swirling water. She could see the glimmer of the mermaid realm far below the surface. "But how can we get there? We can't breathe underwater."

"Actually, you can." Zinzie zipped over to the reeds that grew around the pond. She pulled off the colorful, fuzzy tip of one plant and handed it to Mariposa. "These reeds will give you the ability to breathe underwater. Eat up!"

Mariposa, Zinzie, and the sisters each picked some tips and popped them into their mouths. Suddenly, they knew they could breathe underwater! Into the Waterwhirls they dove.

The friends swam deeper and deeper until they came to the underwater realm. It was beautiful, filled with colorful coral and glistening shells.

"Okay," Rayna said, looking around. "We are here. But where do we find the mermaids?"

"It looks like we found you," said a voice. The girls looked around but could see no one besides themselves.

Just then, where moments before there

had only been coral, two giggling mermaids appeared.

Mariposa turned to the mermaids and tried to ask for help. "We need to find the Ilios antidote. Do you know where it is?"

"Yes," one mermaid replied. But that was all she said.

"Will you *tell* us where to find it?" Mariposa asked.

"No!" the other mermaid responded gleefully. Then she turned back to her mermaid friend. "Anemone, did you see my necklace? It is *exactly* the same color as my eyes when my eyes are this color!"

"Oh, Coral," replied the other mermaid. "Beautiful!"

Mariposa tried again. "I don't think you understand. The fate of our entire city and everyone we know rests on us finding this antidote."

"Oh!" the mermaid named Coral said.

The mermaid called Anemone looked at Mariposa. "Did you bring us something beautiful?"

"No, but I — "

At that moment, Rayna stepped in. She turned to Rayla and said loudly enough that the mermaids could hear, "I think I see

where they are coming from. Do you?"

Rayla nodded. "Why should they help us unless there's something in it for them?" The sisters nodded at each other and then turned back to the mermaids.

"Tell us what you want," Rayna said, "and we will make it happen."

Anemone and Coral looked at each other for a moment. Then they both squealed, "Conkle shells!"

Zinzie explained to the girls that conkle shells were lovely, but difficult to get. The mini-mermaids used them as pillows. However, if anyone woke up sleeping mini-mermaids, they would scream and cry. Then the angry Sea Beast would wake up. And the Sea Beast hated nothing more than being woken up!

Anemone tossed her hair. "We'll be waiting."

With that, Rayna and Rayla led the way toward the mini-merfolk, who were sleeping in a nearby cave. Mariposa and Zinzie swam close behind.

"How do we do this without waking them up?" Mariposa whispered.

"I have an idea," Rayna replied. She grabbed some seaweed leaves and began to tie them into balls. They were about the same size as the conkle shells and would make great pillows!

Zinzie slipped one of her soft ears under the head of a mini-mermaid. While she held the head, Mariposa grabbed the conkle shell and Rayna replaced it with a seaweed pillow. They quietly did the same with another mini-mermaid. Soon they had two conkle shells! Quickly, they began to swim back to the mermaids.

Mariposa looked back as they swam, hoping to see the mini-merfolk sleeping soundly. But one of the seaweed pillows they'd used to replace the conkle shell wasn't tied tightly enough. An end came loose and began to tickle one of the mini-mermaid's noses. The girls and Zinzie stopped swimming and watched, nervously, as the mini-mermaid wrinkled her nose . . . and sneezed.

Startled, the mini-mermaid woke up and began to cry. The girls rushed over and tried to comfort her with soft whispers. But it was no use! Before long, every mini-mermaid was awake — and crying at the top of her lungs.

A huge rumble echoed through the cave. The Sea Beast!

The four friends turned and swam for

their lives as the hungry Sea Beast emerged from his cave. He chased after them, snapping his huge jaws.

"Anemone! Coral!" Rayna cried as they swam. The Sea Beast knew the mermaids had not been the ones who woke him up and left them to watch the chase. Mariposa and her friends tried to swim as fast as they could but the Sea Beast was gaining on them.

"We have your conkle shells!" Rayna called to the mermaids. She stopped swimming and handed one shell to Coral. Mariposa handed the other to Anemone.

Mariposa yelled to the mermaids, "Coral, Anemone! Help us!"

"Do it for the conkle shells!" Rayna called as she swam.

Coral looked down at her shell. "They

are beautiful shells."

The mermaids looked at each other in agreement. "Okay," said Coral. "Let's help."

As the Sea Beast charged Mariposa and her friends, Coral and Anemone swooped in and grabbed them. They swam up through the water quickly with the girls in tow.

At the surface, the girls rejoiced. They were safe!

The mermaids immediately turned to leave.

"Wait!" Rayna called, catching her breath. "What about the Ilios antidote? You said you would tell us where it is!"

Anemone turned back to yell over her shoulder as she splashed away. "In the Cave of Reflection! Head east, then enter the monster's mouth!"

"A monster?" Rayla sighed. "For once, can't we go someplace without a monster?" But the mermaids had disappeared over a nearby waterfall and did not give an answer.

"Let's follow their directions and see what we find." Mariposa turned to Rayna and Rayla as they all flew up into the air. "I'm glad you were here. You handled the mermaids a lot better than I did."

Rayna grinned. "It was easy," she said, looking at her sister. "They reminded us of some fairies we used to know."

Chapter 9

Mariposa and her friends flew east for hours and hours. Would they ever make it to the Cave of Reflection?

"I haven't seen anything." Rayna sighed.

Zinzie tried to smile. "Maybe that's okay! We've had enough monsters for one day. And this one could be even meaner, with long, sharp teeth — like that!" She pointed to a rock off in the distance. The rock looked like a giant, openmouthed monster.

"That's it!" Rayla cried. "The monster!"

Mariposa squinted. "And its mouth is the opening of the cave! That's where we have to go."

Zinzie led the way and they all peeked inside. "So, it's a rock that *looks* like a monster," she said. "I thought we were going to do something really danger— AHH!" Zinzie started to scream but she stopped herself. Before her was a cave filled with sleeping Skeezites!

"We can do this," Mariposa said to her friends. "We've come this far." With that, Mariposa flew quietly inside. Rayna, Rayla, and Zinzie all took deep breaths and followed.

Inside, the cave was scary. Rocks jutted out from the cave walls. The girls had to be careful not to bump into the rocks as they flew. Only a small amount of light crept into

70

the cave, but it was enough that the girls could see that there were snoring Skeezites all around them! They could wake up any minute!

Up ahead, Mariposa spotted a glimmer of light coming from a crevice in a distant cave wall. "The light," she whispered. "It must be that way. Come on." She waved to her friends. But just then —

Yawwwwwwn!

A Skeezite stretched, sat up, and sniffed. "I smell Butterfly Fairy!"

The friends kept going, but as they passed close to another Skeezite, *it* began to wake up.

"Mmmm . . . Yummy Butterfly Fairy." He sniffed the air. "Hmmm . . ."

Mariposa and her friends exchanged horrified looks.

Then another Skeezite woke up and took big sniffs. "Wait a minute," the Skeezite said as he began to sniff the air with interest.

Zinzie acted quickly. She hid behind a rock and used her seed-throwing skills to pelt the Skeezites with bits of gravel. When the Skeezites tried to spot the thrower, they could only see their other Skeezite friends. The Skeezites began to argue with each other and Zinzie motioned for Mariposa and the others to head for the cleft. They were able to fit into the small space and into safety. But just as Zinzie was about to join them, one of the Skeezites spotted her!

Zinzie tried to fly to her friends as quickly as she could but the Skeezites were too fast. They chased her around the cave and nearly got her in their grasp. At the last moment Zinzie slipped through the small crevice in the wall. The Skeezites were too big to follow her and all crashed into the cave wall instead.

The fairies thanked Zinzie for saving them.

"I'll accept payment in Fluttercorn," she responded with a laugh.

The four friends made their way along the crevice toward the light that came from deeper in the cave. Suddenly they passed through an opening and found themselves in a new chamber. But now, instead of a dark and stony cave, they were surrounded by high rounded walls that were crystalline and reflected like mirrors. This cave was like a giant kaleidoscope.

"The Cave of Reflection!" Mariposa

whispered, awestruck.

The girls hadn't gotten far before a tiny, glistening speck flew into their faces. Rayna tried to catch the speck between her hands. But she missed. Instead, it landed on her nose and began to yell at her.

"Watch where you place those mitts," came a tiny voice.

"You're a fairy," cried Mariposa, looking at the tiny person in wonder.

"*The* fairy, as far as anyone trying to enter this cave is concerned," the tiny fairy said as she looked over the group of friends. "One, two, three, four . . . no. Too many."

The four friends were quiet a moment.

"I'll stop, the rest of you go on," Zinzie said at last.

As soon as she spoke, the tiny fairy waved her arm. A barrier slid down from the top of the cave, trapping Zinzie on one side and Mariposa, Rayna, and Rayla on the other.

Mariposa and the sisters waved to Zinzie and did as they were told, flying along the mirrored walls.

As they flew, Rayla whispered, "Do you think it's smart to follow her?"

"I don't think we have a choice," Mariposa said. "This is where the mermaids said we had to go, right?"

Then Mariposa's *reflection* turned and answered! "Yes, it's exactly where they said you had to go."

Mariposa jumped and yelped.

All three fairies turned to face the wall. Their reflections smiled and waved all on their own. Rayna's reflection grinned and said, "It's not *that* weird, is it?" The girls

could hardly believe it!

Before they could figure out what was going on, they turned a corner and the tiny fairy spun around to face them again. "Only two of you can continue," she stated.

"If I stop here, will *she* go away?" Rayla asked, looking over at her reflection.

Rayla's reflection smirked and said, "There's only one way to find out, right?"

Rayla thought for a moment and then turned to her friends. "I'll stay."

Immediately, another wall slammed down. Rayla was left on the other side, as Mariposa and Rayna continued on.

Before long, Rayna's reflection began whispering to her. "This is important — too important to leave to a nothing like Mariposa."

Rayna's jaw dropped. "I never said that!"

"Just ignore it," Mariposa urged. "It's some sort of test."

Then Mariposa's reflection piped up. "Was that advice? From a fairy too unsure of herself to even go to a party?"

Mariposa didn't have a chance to say anything before they turned around another corner. Like before, the small fairy spun to face them. "Only one can continue."

Rayna's reflection leaned forward and spoke in an eager tone. "Go! Think about the glory! Think about the rewards! Think about the prince! Do you really want Mariposa to get all that instead?"

Mariposa's reflection nodded, pointing at Mariposa. "She's right," it said. "Rayna should go. You'll only fail if you try."

Mariposa turned to face Rayna. "Rayna . . ."

Rayna shook her head. "You're the one who can do this, Mariposa. I'm sure of it," she said confidently. Then she turned to the tiny fairy. "I want to stay back."

For the third time, a wall slid down between the girls. The fairy turned and continued on, and Mariposa followed.

Finally, the tiny fairy led Mariposa into

a chamber full of beautiful, bright stars.

The tiny fairy faced Mariposa yet again. "These stars hide many things," she said, gesturing. "One of them is the antidote you seek. You have one chance to choose."

Mariposa quickly scanned the stars above her. "That's impossible! How can I choose one star?" She took a deep breath and thought for a moment. "Wait a minute . . . patterns! The stars always make patterns."

With that in mind, she scanned the specks of light. Almost immediately, she spotted the Archer. Mariposa narrowed her eyes and studied the stars carefully. The Archer pointed to a small star, off by itself.

Mariposa's reflection followed her line

of vision. "That? That little star doesn't fit in with anything else in the sky. It's meaningless!"

"It *doesn't* fit in," Mariposa agreed. A small smile spread across her face. "But that doesn't make it meaningless at all. Every star is there for a reason! They don't have to fit in with the other stars to be important. They just have to be themselves."

Mariposa thought for one more moment. Then she reached out and pointed to the star. As she did she saw a magical dust fall from the star into her hand where suddenly the flower of the Ilios antidote appeared.

"It was the one star off by itself that made all the difference. You knew this in your heart, but it's time you saw it in yourself," the tiny fairy said.

The room began to spin around Mariposa, a bright whirl of colors. The colors grew thicker, brighter, and spun faster. When the chamber stopped spinning, Mariposa looked herself over. She had been transformed! Her wings had always been beautiful, but now they were much larger and sparkled brilliantly.

Mariposa looked at the tiny fairy, stunned. "Thank you," was all she could say.

Suddenly the magical walls of the cave slid away, and Rayna, Rayla, and Zinzie appeared, carried to Mariposa's side by a magical wind. The three friends all gaped at Mariposa's fabulous wings.

"Whoa!" Zinzie said. "Look at your wings."

"Mariposa," said Rayla, "they are beautiful."

The tiny fairy nodded, smiling. "Now go. My winds will carry you and your friends back to Flutterfield."

The winds caught Mariposa, too, and she was swept off with her friends. They had to get back to the palace in time to save the queen!

Chapter 10

Back at the palace, Queen Marabella's magical lights were fading quickly. Henna and Lord Gastrous stayed close to the castle huddled under the last lights in Flutterfield with a small group of palace guards.

"We are doomed, Henna," Lord Gastrous whispered, gazing up at the palace.

"You might be right, Lord Gastrous. It looks like we are about to run out of time," Henna replied quietly.

"You must go join the others and hide

in the root neighborhood," Lord Gastrous told her.

"No," Henna said. "I will stay with the queen to the end."

Just then Prince Carlos flew out of the darkness.

"Prince Carlos!" Lord Gastrous cried. "Where have you been?"

The prince ignored the question and stepped toward Henna. "Perhaps it is Henna who should explain."

"Excuse me?" Henna said, incredulous.

"*She* is behind this! *You* poisoned the queen," the prince accused.

Lord Gastrous moved closer to Henna. "This is ridiculous," he said. "Henna has done nothing to hurt the queen."

"Then perhaps she'd like to explain *this*," said the prince, holding up the vial that he filled in her lair. "We followed you to your lair, Henna. We saw you with the Skeezites. We found the Ilios!"

Lord Gastrous looked at Henna in shock. "You mean —"

"Yes, Lord Gastrous," Henna admitted with an evil smile. "This is all because of me."

Lord Gastrous called the guards and then turned back to Henna. "How could you, Henna? We will all be eaten by the Skeezites!"

"Will we?" Henna asked, and then flew out of view. The others tried to see where she had gone and were dismayed when they spotted her returning — on the back of a Skeezite! Other ravenous Skeezites were close by as she flew.

"Time for your feast, my little friends!"

Henna cried.

The Skeezites flew forward as the fairies watched in horror. Prince Carlos reached desperately into his pocket and pulled out a Thistleburst pod that Willa had given him. Carefully, he poured some of the Ilios into the pod and it began to give off a great light.

The Skeezites howled and covered their eyes in pain, but Henna soothed them. "Fear not, my little Skeezites, one little light cannot hold you *all* back."

"How about a hundred?" came a voice. Willa flew into view, a pack of Flutterpixies behind her. Each was carrying a pod of light.

Henna narrowed her eyes. "An admirable effort. But you can't hold us off forever. So when the queen succumbs to my poison and the lights go out —"

"*Your* poison?" a voice cried.

It was Mariposa! She flew in clutching the Ilios antidote in her hand. Rayna, Rayla, and Zinzie fluttered to her side.

Henna spotted the flower in Mariposa's hand, and her lip curled up into a sneer. "Get her!" she yelled to the Skeezites.

The Skeezites lunged for Mariposa, but before they could do anything, Rayna, Rayla, and Zinzie jumped in their path.

"Go!" Rayna called to Mariposa. "We'll use the lights to hold back the Skeezites."

Mariposa sped into the palace as fast as her wings would take her. She burst into the queen's room but Henna caught up to her before she could get close enough to the queen and grabbed the flower from her hand.

"In less than one minute, the queen's

life force will fade away." Henna chuckled. "Join me, Mariposa. You'll be adored by every single fairy who lives in Flutterfield. Finally you'll fit in."

As Mariposa stared at Henna in shock, she spotted a Flutterpixie flying behind her. She was trying to get the Ilios antidote away from Henna. While Henna kept trying to convince Mariposa to join her, the Flutterpixie was finally able to grab the flower. She zipped to Mariposa and dropped it into her hand.

Now that Mariposa had the antidote, she began beating her new, huge wings and moving toward the queen. "I don't need that anymore, Henna!" she cried as she reached out and held the antidote to the queen's face.

The queen had only taken a single breath

of the antidote when Henna flew up and snatched the flower out of Mariposa's hand. "Too little, too late, Mariposa," she said, laughing. Then she crushed the flower in her hand and destroyed it.

Mariposa gasped. Had the queen gotten enough? Would she recover? Or was Flutterfield lost forever?

As if in answer to her question, the lights began to dim. "Flutterfield is mine!" Henna said gleefully.

But then, just as quickly, the lights began to grow brighter. Mariposa suddenly felt hope flicker inside her, growing as the brightness of the lights grew stronger. And as Mariposa's hope grew, Henna's face began to show fear. Suddenly, the queen gasped and awoke. And as she did, the lights of the palace became brilliantly lit.

Outside the palace, Mariposa's friends and the rest of the Butterfly Fairies were still fighting off the evil Skeezites. But at that moment, the magical lights of Flutterfield burst on, bright and glowing in the darkness.

Mariposa and Henna looked on as the queen began to focus on the room around her. "Henna," she said, laying eyes on her lady in waiting. She looked confused as she tried to remember what had happened and how she had wound up in her bed. "You . . . " she said. But then clarity spread across her face. "You!"

Henna looked frightened. "Your Majesty, I can explain. You know, the funniest thing happened . . . " But before she could invent an explanation, she spotted a Skeezite at the window. She called for it and, as it drew near, she jumped on its back. As she rode into the night and disappeared, she called back over her shoulder, "This isn't over, Flutterfield! I will be back!" And then she was gone.

"I have a feeling there is a lot I need to know," the queen said, turning to Mariposa. "Can you help me?"

"*I* can explain," said Prince Carlos, as he entered the room. "It's a long story, but it all starts with the bravery of Mariposa."

☘   ☘   ☘

Later that night, the palace glowed with twinkling lights. Queen Marabella stood at the head of the crowded ballroom. She was back to her strong, beautiful self and had Prince Carlos at her side. Mariposa, Willa, Rayna, Rayla, Zinzie, and the Flutterpixie who saved the antidote faced them, their cheeks glowing.

"In thanks for your great bravery," the queen announced, "I present you with these gifts."

The queen gave each of them a lovely flower wreath.

The group of friends all turned and faced the audience of fairies and friends. A great cheer arose and they knew that all was well in Flutterfield once more.

Afterword

"And from that day forward, Mariposa always felt that she belonged in Flutterfield. She now knew the most beautiful thing to be is yourself," Elina told Bibble.

Bibble's eyes widened. "But I want to hear more! Does Zinzie stay in Flutterfield?"

"I don't know if Zinzie leaves Flutterfield or not. But don't you have to leave to see Dizzle soon?" She paused. "Oh, wait! That's right — you're not going to go."

Bibble looked shocked. "Of course I'm going to go!"

"You're not worried about fitting in with

Dizzle's friends?" Elina asked.

"Are you kidding? I'm Bibble and being myself is all I need to do!"

Just then, a voice came from outside. "Bibble! Oh, Bibble!"

"Yes?" Bibble said as he flew outside. "Dizzle! You're here!"

"Yes," Dizzle said as she flew up to Bibble. "I brought my friends to meet you." Dizzle gestured behind her to a small group of tiny flying—

"Flutterpixies!"cried Bibble. Elina came outside and joined Bibble. "Dizzle's friends are Flutterpixies," Bibble said to Elina.

"Wow, yes, Bibble, they are," Elina said, smiling.

Dizzle introduced Bibble to her friends. Bibble thanked Elina for her story and then she and Dizzle flew off to enjoy the day with the Flutterpixies.